For Becca, Elinor, Simon, Teddy, and Hazel-Bean

First edition 2016

Library of Congress Catalog Card Number 2015937114
ISBN 978-0-7636-6972-0

16 17 18 19 20 21 CCP 10 9 8 7 6 5 4 3 2 1

Printed in Shenzhen, Guangdong, China

This book was typeset in Caudex.
The illustrations were created digitally.

Candlewick Press
99 Dover Street
Somerville, Massachusetts 02144

visit us at www.candlewick.com

SHRUNKEN
TREASURES

Literary Classics, Short, Sweet, and Silly

SCOTT NASH

CANDLEWICK PRESS

Introducing: THE VERSIZER!

The book you are holding in your hands is a marvel of squishy science. After many years of mulling and figuring, I have developed a device called the Versizer that will transform lengthy novels, myths, and epic poems into delightful nuggets of nonsense. *Moby-Dick,* the *Odyssey, Frankenstein,* and *Hamlet* are among the greatest stories ever written, but they are thousands of words long and weigh up to five pounds! The Versizer uses a mixture of rare elements of style, spice, and illustration to carefully and painlessly reduce big, thick, voluminous literary works to children's verse.

What's more, the process does no damage to the original text, which can be un-shrunk any time you like.

I hope that you enjoy these Versized "shrunken treasures" and urge you to recite and sing them often till you are old enough to read the more weighty classics yourself.

Contents

Frankenstein

Miss Mary made a monster named Dr. Frankenstein.
That monster made another of very strange design.

Its skin was sickly yellow; it had black lips and eyes.
As homely as a scarecrow, it stood near eight feet high.

The two of them were awful and bickered endlessly;
In church or at the table, they acted monstrously!

So Mary called a timeout and thus split up the two:
The monster fled to woodlands, the doc to a mountain view.

But when they reunited, their conduct was much worse.
They jousted and recited all sorts of nonsense verse.

Miss Mary had two monsters that she could not control,
So she sent them packing away to the North Pole.

From then on, life was peaceful,
and Mary gladly took
To sitting at her table,
surrounded by her books . . .

While on a million acres of frozen snowy white,
Two wild and rowdy monsters brawl late into the night.

Moby-Dick

(to the tune of "Mary Had a Little Lamb")

Ahab had a wooden leg,
    wooden leg,
    wooden leg;
Ahab had a wooden leg—
    he got it from a whale.

The whale's name was Moby Dick,
    Moby Dick,
    Moby Dick;
The whale's name was Moby Dick.
    His skin was oh so pale.

Ahab sailed the rolling sea,
    rolling sea,
    rolling sea;
Ahab sailed the rolling sea,
    searching for a spout.

He bumped into a whale of blue,
    whale of blue,
    whale of blue;
He bumped into a whale of blue
    and so began to pout.

He sailed the seas for twenty years,
 twenty years,
 twenty years;
He sailed the seas for twenty years
 and saw a million fish.

He met up with an albatross,
 albatross,
 albatross;
He met up with an albatross,
 who granted him his wish.

Ahab shouted, "Thar she blows!
 Thar she blows!
 Thar she blows!"
Ahab shouted, "Thar she blows!"
 and pulled his ship aside.

Moby offered up his back,
 up his back,
 up his back;
Moby offered up his back
 and gave Ahab a ride.

Jane Eyre

(to the tune of "Three Blind Mice")

Poor Jane Eyre,
  poor Jane Eyre.
Orphan was she,
  orphan was she.
She had to live with
  her wicked old aunt.
Her two awful cousins
  would tease Jane and taunt.
Can you imagine a worse life?
  I can't.
Poor Jane Eyre.

Life was cruel,
  life was cruel.
When Jane grew up,
  when Jane grew up,
She landed a job
  as a governess
For a brooding gent
  whose life was a mess
And lived in a big
  haunted mansion, no less!
Life was cruel.

Things got worse,
  things got worse.
Thrown out was she,
  thrown out was she.
They shipped her away
  to a boarding school
Where students were nasty
  and teachers were cruel
And all they were fed
  was stale bread and gruel.
Things got worse.

Such a mess,
  such a mess.
Sad, haunted man;
  That haunted man.
The house was spooky
  and Jane was afraid.
The attic was home
  to a crazy old maid
Who threatened the gent
  (and Jane if she stayed).
Such a mess!

A Thousand and One Nights

Once there was a sultan's cat
   that weighed four hundred pounds.
This tiger guarded home and hearth
   when no one was around.

The sultan was afraid of mice—
   their mere sight made him pale—
So Big Cat hunted tiny game
   and brought his boss their tails.

A mouse was pinned beneath his paw,
   fearing for her life.
(The tiger ate one mouse each day,
   though rarely ever twice.)

He held the mouse up by the tail
   and looked at her with boredom.
(Munching mice was not his fave;
   it was expected of him.)

The tiger opened up his jaws,
   about to pop her in—
When Mousie squeaked, "Close Sesame!"
   her voice both brave and thin.

"What's that you said?" exclaimed the cat.
   "Your weird words mess me up.
What sort of thing is *that* to say
   as I'm about to sup?"

"The words are taken from a tale
   of derring-do and treasure,
And if you spare my life tonight,
   I'll tell it for your pleasure."

The cat said, "You're a spicy mouse—
alluring, strange, and odd."
"You flatter me," proclaimed the mouse.
"My name's Scheherazade."

"I like my treasure," said the cat,
    "but stories even more so.
Now, tell this tale of derring-do.
    I'll save you for tomorrow."

Scheherazade then told a tale
    of forty thieving hoods:
"Those lawless scoundrels filled a cave
    with pricey stolen goods.

"The cave door was enchanted,
    impossible to see,
Until the big thief said the words
    Open Sesame!

"Through the magic of those words,
    the stone cliff opened wide,
Revealing all the riches that
    the cavern held inside.

"Now it's time to introduce our
    good guy, Ali Baba,
Who was an honest, peaceful man,
    not a crooked robber.

"Behind a boulder near the cave,
    poor Ali was hidden,
Fearing that if he was caught, his
    end was almost certain.

"Those crooks did not discover him,
    so once they rode away,
Ali stood before the cave
    and knew just what to say!

"From that day on, Mr. Ali B.
    became a wealthy man,
For with his treasure from the cave,
    he also made a plan:

"*Be giving to your loved ones,
    and kind to those in need;
Strive to be both rich and wise,
    unlike those forty thieves.*"

"Tell me more!" the tiger roared,
    childish and demanding.
"I must know what happens next.
    That cannot be the ending!"

Mousie smiled, shook her head,
   and squeaked, "That's all for now.
I must go home, but will return
   tomorrow night, I vow."

That didn't sit well with the cat,
   who grabbed the storyteller.
"Gimme the rest or I'll digest
   your volume!" roared the tiger.

"So, eat me," sighed the clever mouse,
   "but that would bring an end
To all my spicy, tasty tales.
   It's up to you, my friend."

The tiger checked his temperature.
   "I guess I'm not that angry.
I'll set you free if you agree
   to tell me the whole story."

Next evening at the story hour,
   the mouse had not arrived.
The tiger felt that he'd been tricked,
   which hurt his feline pride.

He couldn't eat; he couldn't rest.
   The clock struck half past eight.
As it did, the mouse ran in.
   "So sorry that I'm late!"

The pussycat was overjoyed.
   He curled up on the bed
With his enchanting storyteller
   perched upon his head.

When Mousie finished that night's tale
   and headed toward the door,
She said, "I'll come back every night
   and tell one thousand more."

Hamlet

A great Dane was Hamlet.
   He lived in Elsinore
And seemed quite mad
   for digging holes,
Though none could say what for!

He dug one in the garden,
   he dug one on the coast,
And one time, near
   the castle gate,
He dug up the king's ghost.

The ghost would not leave Hamlet—
    onto his tail he clung.
He then decreed
    that Hamlet dig
A hole for everyone.

He dug one for Polonius—
    a rash, intruding fool!
But for the fair
    Ophelia,
He dug a swimming pool.

So he dug holes for nobles,
    for vain and wealthy yokels,
And for his mother,
    Queen Gertrude,
And Claudius, his uncle.

Then halfway through the digging
    of hole bazillion one,
Hamlet finally
    said to all:
"This isn't any fun!"

On that day he ran away
    and found a quiet knoll.
He sniffed the grass,
    the trees, and sea
And dug himself a hole.

21

Don Quixote

An elderly gent from La Mancha
Read too many tales of adventure.
He left his armchair
And decided to wear
Some armor along with his dentures!

He perturbed the horse in his stable,
Who was neither desirous nor able
To carry a knight
Whose most epic fight
Was reading small print on a label.

Don Quixote set off on his quest,
Inviting a friend as his guest:
Sancho Panza by name,
On a donkey he came.
As knight's squire, he would give it his best.

They encountered a wind-powered mill
That insulted the knight from a hill.
Quixote was brave—
He'd strike down the knave!—
He charged and went in for the kill.

The giant stood calm and unrattled
As knight upon horse charged in battle.
With four arms it swung
And Don Q was flung
Up high and clear out of his saddle.

Good Sancho collected his master
From the scene of defeat and disaster.
He bandaged Don's head,
And it has been said
That the knight chased no windmills thereafter.

The Metamorphosis

When Gregor awoke on the ceiling,
He had a prickly feeling.
He realized, surveying his rug,
That he had turned into a bug.

He sat at the table for breakfast.
His parents seemed almost insect-ist—
They despaired and were thoroughly grossed
When Gregor poured juice on his toast.

They said, "Go and change up your species!"
Their words simply tore him to pieces.
He balled up his sadness and gloom
And rolled it upstairs to his room.

"I've got to be me!" Gregor said,
As he scuttled, quick, under the bed.
He hid in the dark and he pouted
And grumbled, "I'll never be outed!"

His sister played violin
Outside of the room he was in.
And though she said nothing at all,
She coaxed Gregor out to the hall.

She was happy to see her bug brother.
They scurried outside together.
And as the sun set that odd day,
Said Gregor, "I'll dance while you play!"

Remembrance of Things Past
Marcel Proust

In Marcel Proust's *Remembrance of Things Past*, a man dips a sweet cake into a cup of tea—and unleashes a torrent of memories, which fill the three thousand pages of this highly regarded work. Although I have yet to finish reading this mammoth novel, I was able to craft a rhyme from what I have read, which, I am proud to say, is the shortest in the book.